# YASMIN

## The Librarian

written by
### SAADIA FARUQI

illustrated by
### HATEM ALY

PICTURE WINDOW BOOKS
a capstone imprint

To Mariam for inspiring me, and Mubashir
for helping me find the right words—S.F.

To my sister, Eman, and her amazing girls,
Jana and Kenzi—H.A.

Yasmin is published by Picture Window Books, an imprint of Capstone.
1710 Roe Crest Drive
North Mankato, Minnesota 56003
www.capstonepub.com

Text copyright © 2021 by Saadia Faruqi.
Illustrations copyright © 2021 by Capstone.

Library of Congress Cataloging-in-Publication Data
Names: Faruqi, Saadia, author. | Aly, Hatem, illustrator. Title: Yasmin
the librarian / written by Saadia Faruqi ; illustrated by Hatem Aly.
Description: North Mankato, Minnesota : Picture Window Books,
[2021] | Series: Yasmin | Audience: Ages 5-7. | Audience: Grades K-1.
| Summary: It is library day and helper Yasmin is busy shelving
books, but suddenly she discovers that her own special book is
missing prompting her to calmly retrace her steps. Identifiers: LCCN
2020038986 (print) | LCCN 2020038987 (ebook) | ISBN 9781515882596
(hardcover) | ISBN 9781515883722 (paperback) | ISBN 9781515892496
(pdf) | ISBN 9781515893257 (kindle edition) Subjects: CYAC: Libraries—
Fiction. | Schools—Fiction. | Lost and found possessions—Fiction. |
Pakistani Americans—Fiction. | Muslims—United States—Fiction.
Classification: LCC PZ7.1.F373 Yh 2021 (print) | LCC PZ7.1.F373 (ebook)
|DDC [E]—dc23 LC record available at https://lccn.loc.gov/2020038986
LC ebook record available at https://lccn.loc.gov/2020038987

Editorial Credits:
Editor: Kristen Mohn; Designer: Kay Fraser; Production Specialist:
Tori Abraham

Design Elements:
Shutterstock: LiukasArt,

# TABLE OF CONTENTS

# CHAPTER 1

# The Helper

Yasmin's class lined up to go to the library. It was the last hour of the day. Everyone was tired.

Except for Yasmin. She was excited. She had a book to show the librarian. And it was her day to be helper!

"Come in, come in!" called Mrs. Kogo, the librarian. "The library is waiting for you!"

The library was big and sunny. There were shelves of books everywhere.

"Yasmin, what's that under your arm?" Mrs. Kogo asked.

"I brought my favorite book to show you. It's about cats. My baba gave it to me!" Yasmin said.

Mrs. Kogo's desk was piled high with books.

"How nice! We'll look at it after our library work is done."

She smiled at Yasmin.

"I see that you're my helper today. If we work together, we can put all the books back in no time!"

Yasmin nodded. "I'm ready to work!"

# CHAPTER 2

# Busy with Books

Mrs. Kogo showed Yasmin how to shelve books.

"The storybooks go in order by the author's last name," Mrs. Kogo said. She showed Yasmin the alphabet signs on the shelves. "As long as you know your ABCs you'll be fine."

Yasmin piled all the books in
a cart and began shelving. A,
then B, then C . . . all the way up
to Z. She even found an author
with the last name Ahmad, just
like her!

Emma walked up. "Yasmin, I can't find the book I want," she complained.

Yasmin checked the author's last name. It started with a G.

"Right there!" Yasmin pointed.

"Thanks, Yasmin!" Emma said.

When the books were all shelved, Mrs. Kogo asked Yasmin to tidy up the tables and chairs.

Ali needed help too.

"Yasmin, do you know where the bookmarks are?" he asked.

Yasmin found the box on Mrs. Kogo's desk. "Here you go!"

Finally, all Yasmin's tasks were finished. Now she could show Mrs. Kogo her special book.

But . . . where was it? Yasmin realized she didn't have it anymore.

"My kitaab!" She felt like crying. Where was her book from Baba?

# CHAPTER 3

# The Special Book

Yasmin took a deep breath and looked around. She'd worked in so many places in the library. How would she find her book? She would have to go back to each one and look.

First, she went to Mrs. Kogo's desk. The box of bookmarks was there, but no special book.

Then she went to the shelves. She checked each section, A through Z. No special book there, either.

Oh no! Had someone

accidentally taken it?

Suddenly, Yasmin heard

Mrs. Kogo's voice. She was

talking about animals.

Yasmin turned. Her class was sitting on the carpet. Story time had started. Mrs. Kogo was reading Yasmin's special book from Baba!

She hurried toward them and found a seat next to Emma.

"Yasmin, this book is fantastic," Emma whispered. "Cats are so cool!"

"I know," Yasmin whispered back with a smile.

Soon, the bell rang. Mrs. Kogo stopped reading. "Thank you for sharing this book with the class, Yasmin!"

"But we didn't get to finish it!" Ali said.

"I have an idea," Yasmin said. "I'll let Mrs. Kogo borrow my book for the week. Then everyone will have a chance to read it!"

Mrs. Kogo smiled. "You make a great librarian, Yasmin!"

# Think About It, Talk About It

❋ What special item might you take to school for show-and-tell or to share with a friend or teacher? Why is it special to you?

❋ Have you ever lost something important? If you were Yasmin in this story, what would you have done? Imagine what might have happened if Yasmin couldn't find her book.

❋ Have you ever been asked to help a teacher with tasks, like Mrs. Kogo asked Yasmin to do? How did this make you feel? Think of a time when helping was fun. Think of another time when helping was a chore. Why were they different?

# Learn Urdu with Yasmin!

Yasmin's family speaks both English and Urdu. Urdu is a language from Pakistan. Maybe you already know some Urdu words!

**baba** (BAH-bah)—father

**hijab** (HEE-jahb)—scarf covering the hair

**jaan** (jahn)—life; a sweet nickname for a loved one

**kameez** (kuh-MEEZ)—long tunic or shirt

**kitaab** (kee-TAHB)—book

**lassi** (LAH-see)—a yogurt drink

**nana** (NAH-nah)—grandfather on mother's side

**nani** (NAH-nee)—grandmother on mother's side

**salaam** (sah-LAHM)—hello

**shukriya** (shuh-KREE-yuh)—thank you

# Pakistan Fun Facts

Yasmin and her family are proud of their Pakistani culture. Yasmin loves to share facts about Pakistan!

Islamabad

PAKISTAN

Pakistan is on the continent of Asia, with India on one side and Afghanistan on the other.

The word Pakistan means "land of the pure" in Urdu and Persian.

Many languages are spoken in Pakistan, including Urdu, English, Saraiki, Punjabi, Pashto, Sindhi, and Balochi.

Malala Yousafzai from Pakistan won a Nobel Peace Prize at age 17. She is the youngest person to win a Nobel.

The common leopard, snow leopard, and Asiatic cheetah are three types of wild cats that live in Pakistan.

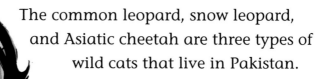

# Make a Yasmin Bookmark!

## SUPPLIES:

- ruler
- cardstock or stiff paper
- scissors
- pencil
- tracing or lightweight paper
- tape
- colored pencils, crayons, or markers

## STEPS:

1. Cut a 2 inch x 6 inch piece of cardstock.

2. Draw Yasmin on the cardstock, or use the tracing paper to trace the Yasmin figure shown here.

3. If you traced, cut out your tracing and tape it to the cardstock.

4. Use pencils, crayons, or markers to color Yasmin and fill in details.

5. Use your new Yasmin bookmark to save your place in your favorite book!

## About the Author

Saadia Faruqi is a Pakistani American writer, interfaith activist, and cultural sensitivity trainer featured in *O Magazine*. She is author of two middle grade novels, *A Place at the Table* and *A Thousand Questions*. She is also editor-in-chief of *Blue Minaret*, an online magazine of poetry, short stories, and art. Besides writing books, she also loves reading, binge-watching her favorite shows, and taking naps. She lives in Houston, Texas, with her husband and children.

Hatem Aly is an Egyptian-born illustrator whose work has been published all over the world. He currently lives in beautiful New Brunswick, Canada, with his wife, son, and more pets than people. When he is not dipping cookies in a cup of tea or staring at blank pieces of paper, he is usually drawing, reading, or daydreaming. You can see his art in books that earned multiple starred reviews and positions on the *NYT* Best-Sellers list, such as *The Proudest Blue* (with Ibtihaj Muhammad & S.K. Ali) and *The Inquisitor's Tale* (with Adam Gidwitz), a Newbery Honor winner.

# Join Yasmin on all her adventures!

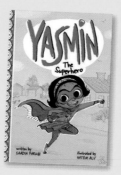